Sophie Johnson:
DETECTIVE
GENIUS

Morag Hood and Ella Okstad

SIMON & SCHUSTER

London   New York   Sydney   Toronto   New Delhi

My name is Sophie Johnson and I am a **detective genius.**

WITHDRAWN FROM STOCK

UNICORNS

I solve crimes and battle baddies.
And I sometimes eat my vegetables.

I had to study really hard to
learn how to be a detective,

but luckily,

I knew where to look.

This is my new assistant, Bella.

She's not a very good assistant, actually.

We are the same age,

but I am definitely smarter than her.

Bella's not very keen on detecting outdoors . . .

and she's a very fussy eater.

But I don't have time to teach Bella
how to be a detective . . .

. . . I have a lot of Very Important Things to be doing.

There has been a terrible crime, and I, Sophie Johnson: Detective Genius will find out who the criminal is!

I get straight to work, arresting suspects and taking fingerprints, but Bella doesn't understand what being a detective is all about.

She just keeps trying to show me things that I know can't possibly be important.

While I am very busy detecting things,

Bella just shouts about nothing all day long.

She is always pestering me to play silly games with her, but I won't be distracted. I have interviews to do.

I SPY

CLUES VOL II

CLUES VOL I

DETECTIVES

Catching criminals doesn't happen without a lot of hard work, you know . . .

. . . and Bella is no help,

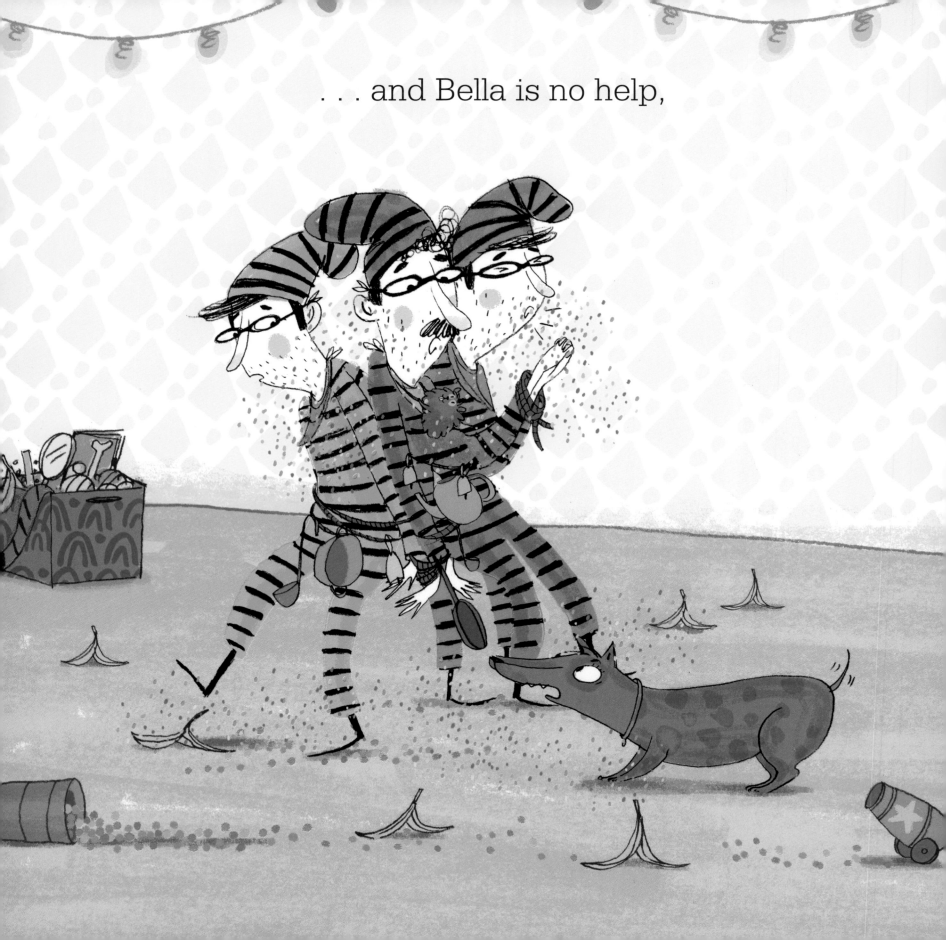

no help at all.

Bella wouldn't notice if a crime happened

right under her nose.

Really, it's a good job I'm here, otherwise there would be criminals **everywhere**.

That's why they need me –
Sophie Johnson, Detective Genius.